My name is Hédi, and I am going to tell you about my childhood. About being a happy child in a happy place. What happened later on is hard to talk about and hard to hear about. Still, I want to tell you and I want you to listen. People can do such evil things, but they can do good things as well. We all have a choice: we can choose to do what is good.

— hédi fried

the story of

Bodri

Hédi Fried

illustrated by
Stina Wirsén

translated by **linda schenck**

eerdmans books for young readers

grand rapids, michigan

Bodri was my best friend. His coat was soft and brown.
My little sister thought Bodri belonged to her. Mother said
he belonged to all of us.

But Bodri and I knew that most of all, he was mine.

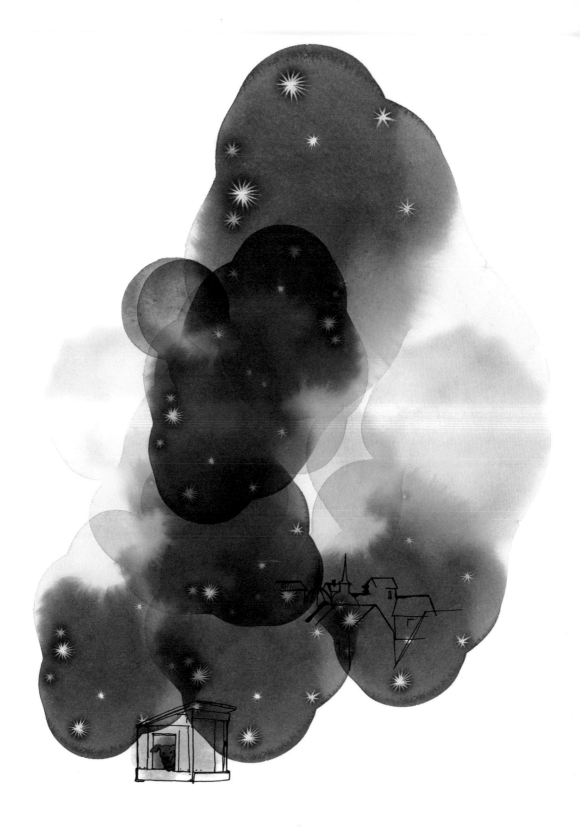

Bodri was our guard dog. I slept well at night
because I knew Bodri was watching over our family
and our little town.

My friend Marika lived on the other side of the fence.
We shared lots of secrets, and we had so much fun together.
We both loved dogs and whipped cream and climbing right
up to the top of the walnut tree. I loved playing with Marika,
and Bodri loved playing with Marika's dog Bandi.

We knew all the best hiding places, where to find
the juiciest plums, and that we had to watch out
for the big dog on the other side of the street.

Marika and I were almost the same height, and we were both really good at whistling. She ran faster than I did, but I was better at reading. If we ever argued, we made up almost right away. Looking at us, we were very much alike. We both had scabby knees and new front teeth.

The only difference between us was that we said different prayers. Marika went to church, and I went to synagogue. I was Jewish. Marika wasn't.

One day I heard a man's voice shouting on our radio in a foreign language. His name was Adolf Hitler.

Mother said: *He won't come here.*

Father said: *We haven't done anything wrong. We don't need to be afraid.*

War broke out and soldiers came to our town. The soldiers took orders from Hitler, and we took orders from the soldiers. I was no longer allowed to play outside. I was no longer allowed to go out with Bodri. I was no longer allowed to play with Marika.

Hitler hated me even though he didn't know me. He hated me and my family because we were Jewish. It didn't make any sense.

Marika and I still played together anyway, since we could crawl through a hole in the fence. We played under her cherry tree or under our plum tree.

One day, even though we weren't allowed, we snuck out to the park, our lovely park with all the climbing trees and hiding places. For a little while things felt normal again.

But then we saw a sign, a big shiny sign on our bench,
the bench where we'd sat so many times—Marika, Bodri,
Bandi, and I. *Für Juden verboten.* No Jews allowed.

After that, we didn't dare to play outside anymore.
We had to stay indoors. The grown-ups said that things
would soon get better. It was only a matter of time.

But things didn't get better.

One day, Hitler decided that we Jewish people were
no longer allowed to live in our homes.

Then where are we going to live? I asked Mother.
She didn't know.

Father's hands trembled as he packed our bags. Mother was
pale. It had never occurred to me that mothers and fathers
could be afraid. Now I knew that we were in danger.

The soldiers rounded us up. They rounded up my family and all the other Jews. Hitler's soldiers scared us with their weapons and their blank stares.

We passed through the park where Bodri, Bandi, Marika,
and I used to play, past the bench with its shiny new sign, past
our climbing trees and our hiding places.

Suddenly I felt a rough tongue licking my hand . . . Bodri had
been following us, wanting to come along. But the soldiers
kicked him and struck out at him, and he ran away to avoid
more beatings.

He cautiously crept along behind us, all the way to the station,
where my family and I were put onto a train.

The train pulled out, and Bodri ran after it as far as he could. Other abandoned dogs gathered around him. I waved and waved and waved until my Bodri was out of sight . . .

I thought about him every day and every night, about how he was getting along without me. I imagined him and his new dog friends sleeping in the woods, searching for food when they were hungry, helping each other. I imagined him going to Bandi's house and yapping outside the door.

Perhaps Marika would see him through the window and know that he was hungry. Maybe she would sneak out with some bones, and pat his soft fur. I imagined Bodri rushing back to his dog friends to share.

The grown-ups disappeared. We were cold and frightened. We were hungry and thirsty. My sister and I almost died in that camp they took us to. Hitler's prison guards shaved our heads and took our clothes. We had to wear dirty uniforms and hard shoes.

Thinking about Bodri gave me strength. Dreaming about our old life made it possible for me to go on living. When I was hungry, I thought about Bodri; when I was tired, I thought about Bodri; when I missed Mother and Father, I thought about Bodri. Many days passed, and many nights.

Bodri couldn't count the days and nights, but he
watched the trees change into their snowy pajamas.

And then into their soft, lacy green skirts . . .

. . . and even later into long, dark green gowns.

One day, when the trees had already put on their copper-red autumn robes, Bodri heard someone calling his name.

Bodri! Bodri!

He could hardly believe his ears, but when he turned around it was really her!

It was me!

Bodri rushed over to me, jumping up on me, twirling around me, licking me and hugging me and howling with joy! After a while he settled down, looking at me with tears in his eyes, seeing that I wanted to say something.

That was when I told him the war was over.

Adolf Hitler was dead.

I told him about all the evil Hitler had done before the war finally ended, and that many, many people had been murdered. They were murdered even though they had done nothing wrong, just because Hitler had declared that they should die.

But some people, including my little sister Livia and I, survived.

We are here, and we go on telling everyone about what happened.

So that it will never happen again.

hédi fried is a Swedish-Hungarian author, psychologist, and public lecturer. As a teenager she experienced the horrors of the Holocaust in Auschwitz, Bergen-Belsen, and several work camps. Today she speaks internationally on the dangers of racism and the value of democracy.

During one of Hédi's lectures, a six-year-old asked what happened to the family dog, and the seed for *The Story of Bodri* was planted. Hédi's previous books include *The Road to Auschwitz* (University of Nebraska Press) and *Questions I Am Asked about the Holocaust* (Scribe), which was named a USBBY Outstanding International Book. Visit her website at hedifried.se.

stina wirsén is a Swedish designer and artist whose work has been exhibited around the world. She was a staff illustrator for *Dagens Nyheter*, Sweden's largest morning paper, for two decades, and she served as head of the paper's illustration department for ten of those years. Stina and Hédi first met while working on a democracy and human rights project, which started the conversations that fueled this project. *The Story of Bodri* is Stina's first book published in English. She lives in Stockholm, Sweden. Follow Stina on Instagram @stinawirsen or visit her website at stinawirsen.se.

First published in the United States in 2021
by Eerdmans Books for Young Readers,
an imprint of Wm. B. Eerdmans Publishing Co.
Grand Rapids, Michigan

www.eerdmans.com/youngreaders

Text copyright © 2019 Hédi Fried
Illustrations copyright © 2019 Stina Wirsén
Original title: *Historien om Bodri*
First published in 2019 by Natur & Kultur, Stockholm, Sweden 2019
English edition published in agreement with Koja Agency
English language translation copyright © Linda Schenck 2021
All rights reserved

Manufactured in China.

29 28 27 26 25 24 23 22 21   1 2 3 4 5 6 7 8 9

ISBN 978-0-8028-5565-7

A catalog record of this book is available from the Library of Congress.

The cost of this translation was defrayed by a subsidy from
the Swedish Arts Council, gratefully acknowledged.

Illustrations created with watercolor, ink, and digital media